Super Camper Caper

BY JOHN HIMMELMAN

SILVER PRESS

For Unc, who survived the childhoods of my
brothers and me.

—J.H.

Library of Congress Cataloging-in-Publication Data

Himmelman, John.
    The super camper caper / by John Himmelman.
    p. cm.—(The Fix-it family)
    Summary: The Wright family takes an exciting camping trip when
Dad turns their truck into a super camper.
    [1. Camping—Fiction. 2. Inventors—Fiction. 3. Beavers—
Fiction.] I. Title. II. Series: Himmelman,
    John, Fix-it family.
PZ7.H5688Su 1991
[E]—dc20   90-39411
ISBN 0-671-69640-8 (pbk.)   CIP
ISBN 0-671-69636-X (lsb)   AC

1 2 3 4 5 6 7 8 9 0

Produced by Small Packages, Inc.
Copyright © 1991 by John Himmelman and Small Packages, Inc.
All rights reserved. No part of this book may be used
or reproduced in any manner whatsoever without written
permission from the publisher.
Published by Silver Press, a division of
Silver Burdett Press, Inc.
Simon & Schuster, Inc.,
Prentice Hall Bldg., Englewood Cliffs, NJ 07632.
Printed in the United States of America.
10 9 8 7 6 5 4 3 2 1

The Fix-It Family

Orville and Willa Wright

own a fix-it shop.

If something is broken,

they will repair it.

They can fix anything!

They are also inventors.

And their children—

Alexander, Graham, and Belle—

like inventing things, too.

CHAPTER ONE
Going Camping

It was the first morning

of spring vacation.

Willa, Alexander, Graham, and Belle

sat out in the yard.

A huge white sheet hung in front of them.

The sheet covered Orville's

latest invention.

"I think it is a giant weed puller,"
whispered Alexander.

"I'll bet it is a helicopter,"
whispered Graham.

"No, it is an elephant," said Belle.

Everyone chuckled.

"Are you ready to see

my new invention?" asked Orville.

"Yes!" said his family.

Orville pulled off the sheet.

"Surprise!" he shouted.

"I have turned our truck

into a super camper."

"Hooray!" cheered the children.

"We're going camping."

Orville showed them around the camper.

"It has super rubber tires

for bumpy country roads.

"It has a wood stove

for cooking country meals.

And it has comfy cots to sleep on,"

he said proudly.

"But best of all,

it has a pancake flipper!"

Orville loved pancakes

when he went camping.

And this year, he'd even made

his own special maple syrup.

Soon everyone was packed.

They hooked their boat to the camper

and headed down the road.

By the end of the day

they reached the forest.

"This is a nice spot," said Willa.

They spent the evening
telling ghost stories
and toasting marshmallows.

And that night, they slept soundly
in their comfy cots.

Soon it was morning.

"Pancake time!" called Orville.

He set the pancake flipper

on EXTRA HIGH.

"This will be fun," he said.

He hit the switch.

The pancake flipper smashed the pan

right through the roof!

Graham peered through the hole.

"I see rain clouds," he said.

"We are going to get wet."

"If we put the boat on the roof,
it will cover the hole," said Willa.
She and Orville and Graham
lifted the boat onto the camper.
"That will keep the rain out,"
said Orville.

"What if it blows off?" thought Belle.

"I'd better glue it in place."

She grabbed Orville's maple syrup.

"This looks like strong glue!"

she said.

She climbed onto the roof
and poured it over the boat.

Then she joined the others inside.

Orville finished making pancakes.

"Where's my syrup?" he said.

"More important," said Willa,

"where's Alexander?"

CHAPTER TWO
Lost in the Woods

Alexander had gotten up early

to go exploring.

"Spring is here,"

he called to the birds.

"Time to start singing.

"Spring is here,"

he called to the flowers.

"Time to start blooming.

"It is still winter,"

he lied to the mosquitos.

"Keep sleeping."

After a while,

Alexander felt hungry.

"I'd better head back," he thought.

"But which way do I go?"

Alexander was lost.

"I will stay right here,"

he decided.

"Someone will come looking

for me soon."

Someone did come soon.

It was a young opossum.

He looked very frightened.

"Hi, I'm Alexander," said Alexander.

"I'm Davey Possum," said the opossum.

"And I am lost."

"Me, too," said Alexander.

"Why don't you wait with me.

Someone will come soon."

But no one came.

It began to rain.

The forest began to flood.

They went to the top of a hill.

The water rose higher and higher.

Their hill became an island.

"We can swim to safety,"
said Alexander.

"Not me," said Davey.

"I cannot swim."

"Then I will stay here with you,"
said Alexander.

"I'm scared," said Davey.

"Do not be scared," said Alexander.

"Someone will come soon."

But Alexander was scared, too.

Then he saw a large, dark shape.

It was coming toward them.

"What is that?" asked Davey.

"It is my family!" shouted Alexander.

The camper floated upside down

in the water.

The Wrights were paddling

out of the windows.

"Climb aboard," shouted Orville.

Soon Alexander and Davey

were safe inside.

"We were so worried about you!"

said Willa.

"Mom," said Alexander.

"Why is the camper upside down?"

Willa looked at Orville and Belle.
"Because your father makes
the stickiest syrup around,"
she said.

CHAPTER THREE
Up, Up, and Away!

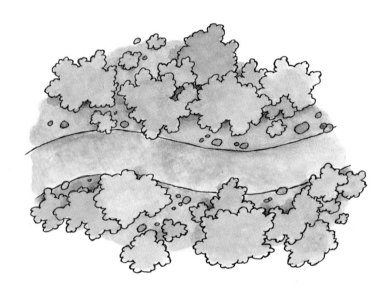

At last the rain stopped.

The sun began to dry the forest.

"We will find your family,"

Orville promised Davey.

"But it will not be easy.

There are so many trees!"

Alexander looked at his father's

pancake flipper.

It gave him an idea.

When he was ready,

he strapped himself to the flipper.

He set it on EXTRA, EXTRA HIGH.

"Fire away!" he shouted.

The pancake flipper

lifted him high above the trees.

"Mom," said Graham,

"I think I just saw Alexander

fly through the air."

"Come down, Alexander," said Willa.

"This flipper is for pancakes.

It is not for young beavers."

"But I can see the whole forest

from here," said Alexander.

"And I found Davey's family, too!"

It did not take long

to reach the Possums.

Davey's family was very happy

to see him again.

The two families became good friends.

They shared ghost stories.

They shared toasted marshmallows.

And in the morning,

Orville made them all pancakes

with his pancake flipper—

set on extra, extra low.

"Let's have jam instead of syrup,"

said Willa.

"Good idea," said Orville.

Finally it was time to leave.

"See you next year,"

said the Possums.

"See you next year,"

said the Wrights.

And they left the forest.

"It will be good to get home,"
said Willa.

"*If* we get home," said Orville.

A great big boulder blocked the road.

"We cannot drive around it,"
said Orville.

"Too bad this camper can't fly,"
said Alexander.

"Hmmm," said Orville.

"Everyone come with me."

They took the big rubber tires

off the camper.

They they tied them to the roof.

"You can get back in the camper now,"

said Orville.

He filled the tires with hot air

from the stovepipe.

Then he joined his family inside.

"Hey, the trees are getting smaller!"

said Belle.

"We're flying!" said Graham.

"There's nothing like
super rubber tires
for bumpy country roads,"
said Orville.
And they laughed
the whole way home.

The End